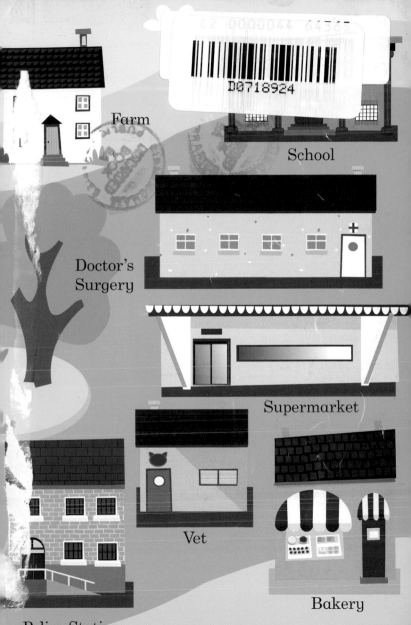

Farm

School

Doctor's Surgery

Supermarket

Vet

Police Station

Bakery

A catalogue record for this book is available from the British Library
Published by Ladybird Books Ltd
80 Strand London WC2R ORL
A Penguin Company

1 3 5 7 9 10 8 6 4 2

© LADYBIRD BOOKS MMIX

ISBN: 978-1-40930-292-6

Printed in China

# Just the Job
# Frank the Farmer

by Ronne Randall

illustrated by Paul Nicholls

"Cock-a-doodle-doo!"
crowed the cockerel.
It was getting-up time
on the farm.
"Come on, Nell!"
said Frank the farmer.
"We've got lots
to do today!"

At breakfast, Frank's wife
Molly was upset. "Peg the cat
is missing," she said.
"I think she's lost!"
"Don't worry," said Frank.
"Nell and I will
find her!"

NELL

PEG

In the farmyard,
Frank thought
he heard a "Miaow!"
"Maybe Peg's in the
henhouse," he said
to Nell.

In the henhouse, Delia and Delilah were feeling very pleased. They had laid two eggs each!

"Cluck! Cluck!" said Delia.

"Cluck! Cluck!" said Delilah.

But where was Peg?

"Maybe Peg's in the pigsty," said Frank. He put some feed in the trough for Primrose and her piglets.

"Oink!" said Primose.

"Squeal, squeeeal!" said her hungry little piglets.

But where was Peg?

"Perhaps Peg
is in the barn,"
said Frank.
He milked Daisy
the cow while
he was in there.
"Moo," said Daisy.
But where was Peg?

MILK

Suddenly, Nell ran over
to the hayloft.

"Woof! Woof! Woof!"
she barked.

"Hopping haystacks!"
said Frank.

"It's Peg!"

"Woof! Woof!" barked Nell.

"Hopping haystacks!"
said Frank.

"You'll never guess what...!"

PEG

27

Soon it was time for tea.
"Hopping haystacks!" said
Frank the farmer.
"What an
exciting day!"
"Woof! Woof!"
agreed Nell.

23

Peg had six fluffy little kittens!

"That's why she came up to the hayloft!" said Frank.

"She wanted to have her babies where it was warm and quiet."

Molly brought Peg a bowl
of Daisy's fresh milk.

"Well done, Peg!"
said Frank.

"Miaow!"
said Peg.

"Mew-mew!"
said her six
new kittens.

Frank found his ladder,
but it was broken!

"I'll have to call Ben the
builder!" he said.

Ben arrived with his ladder.

Frank climbed up to
the hayloft.

Fire Station

Builder's Yard

Train
Station

Florist

Post Office

Toy Shop